Earl's Too Cool for Me

Earl's Too Cool for Me

by Leah Komaiko · illustrated by Laura Cornell

 HarperTrophy

A Division of HarperCollins*Publishers*

EARL'S TOO COOL FOR ME

Text copyright © 1988 by Leah Komaiko
Illustrations copyright © 1988 by Laura Cornell
Printed in Mexico. All rights reserved.

Library of Congress Cataloging-in-Publication Data
Komaiko, Leah.
  Earl's too cool for me/Leah Komaiko ; illustrated by
Laura Cornell. — 1st ed.
    p.   cm.
  Summary: The antics and adventures of cool boy Earl
include riding on the Milky Way, growing a rose from his
fingernails, and swinging with gorillas.
  ISBN 0-06-023281-1.—ISBN 0-06-023282-X (lib. bdg.)
  ISBN 0-06-443245-9 (pbk.)
  (1. Stories in rhyme.)   I. Cornell, Laura, ill.   II. Title.
PZ8.3.K835Ear 1988   87-30803
(E)—dc19   CIP
                                                    AC

First Harper Trophy edition, 1990.

For: Bill, Cool Davy H and Earl's real friend, Laura Geringer
L. K.

For: Big Barbs, Little Neal and Big D.
L. C.

Earl's got a bicycle made of hay.

He takes rides on the Milky Way.

Earl's too cool for me.

Earl's got a hat with a real horse feather.
He wears socks made of chicken leather.

Earl's too cool for me.

Earl knows all the letters in the Zulu alphabet.
He caught wild boars in a butterfly net.

Earl's too cool for me.

Earl's been to France and South Zanzibar.
He drove to China in an egg roll car.

Earl's too cool for me.

Earl grew a rose from his fingernails.

He once turned green for the Prince of Wales.

Earl floats a ship in his bubbly tub.

He taught an octopus how to scrub.

Earl's too cool for me.

Earl swings with gorillas—and when he's tired of that—

He plays jazz with the alley cat.

Earl's too cool for me.

Earl's friendly with the Martians and a few movie stars.

He keeps monster eyes in empty jelly jars.

Earl's too cool for me.

Now here comes Earl,

I'm not cool like he is—

But all he says is ... "Hi."

Yes, Earl's pretty funny, and he's really nice.

He's eight years old and only thrown up twice!

We're cool as cool can be.